I0526826

i

Copyright © 2011 P. A. Navarro

All rights reserved.

www.thegiftgiverstory.com

ISBN: 0615575021
ISBN-13: 978-0615575025 (Hometree Books)

DEDICATION

To my beautiful wife who has stood by me draft after draft.

ACKNOWLEDGMENTS

This book has been the result of the remarkable insight and talent of my knowledgeable mother, Rachel Navarro, my dedicated agent, Danielle Chiotti, and the always willing and capable Plot Ninjas. You guys rock!

The Gift Giver

P. A. Navarro

THE GIFT GIVER

"Tomorrow is the last day of school before Christmas break," said Miss Trickle, holding up a dusty old fedora in front of the class. "Everyone's name is on a slip of paper in this hat, and you will each pick a name and give that person a gift at the end of school tomorrow for our Secret Santa party." The children gasped, delighting in the thought of giving gifts to their friends, and then the teacher leaned over and whispered with a smile. "Remember, the name you pick is a secret."

When the hat came around, Gracie Gimbler reached inside and wished hard for Odella Berg's name. Gracie's family had just moved to town and she was in need of a good friend, and everyone wanted to be Odella's friend because she wore the prettiest clothes, took ballet lessons at Madam Conway's, and she even played the flute! What better way

for Gracie to win her friendship than to give her a gift for the secret Santa?

Alas, Gracie pulled out a piece of paper from the hat and read the name, Rufus Minly.

"Hmph!" Gracie sighed. Rufus was the most ill-mannered, booger-faced, brute-of-a-boy in the class, and Gracie had told him so on more than one occasion. She told him when he kicked Miss Trickle's stack of books over, she told him when he threw a 1st grade boy's ball over the fence, and she told him just the day before when he tried to steal Natalia Lee's lunch. Natalia lived next door to Gracie, but everyone at school just called her Nat. She wore ratty old clothes, and was small even by 2nd grade standards, so it was no wonder Rufus liked to pick on her.

Gracie frowned as she stared down at Rufus' awful name on the slip a paper.

Just as the last person picked a name, the bell rang and everyone jerked out of their chairs and sprinted for the door. Miss Trickle stopped them by saying, "Aaaand…!" They all sat down again, impatiently waiting to hear what the teacher had to say. "The gifts should be homemade or something that you already have that you would like to give to someone else. There should be no money spent on gifts."

After school, the children waited outside for their parents and couldn't help but break Miss Trickle's first rule of the Secret Santa and rumors spread about who pulled whose name out of the hat. Gracie's heart swelled with joy when she overheard Odella say she got Gracie's name. Odella didn't seem very excited about it, but that just made Gracie more determined to win her over. *If I could give Odella just the right gift*, she thought, *I know we could be best friends*. Gracie made up her mind: she just *had* to be Odella's Secret Santa. But how?

Then her eyes widened as she got a spectacular idea.

First she traded Rufus' name to Marcus because they were best friends. Then she traded Cindy's name to Herman, because everyone knew Herman liked Cindy, and finally she convinced Valaria to trade Owen's name for Odella's because Valaria and Owen were cousins.

By the time she got on the bus for home, Odella's name was in Gracie's coat pocket. She smiled broadly knowing that she and the fanciest dresser in school would soon trade gifts and become best friends forever.

When she got home, Gracie looked around her bedroom trying to think of what to give Odella. She knew it had to be something extra special, something that would grab her attention and make her gasp with delight. She poked around the desk, under the bed, and then found inspiration in an unopened moving box full of things Gracie had yet to find a special place for in her room. It was her beading kit.

She picked up the varnished wood box, lifted the gold clasp and peered inside. The kit came complete with a rainbow of colored string, sparkling beads, and red and blue looms—everything needed to make bracelets, necklaces, and friendship rings. Gracie had dreamed of owning the kit for months and months, but her mother always said, "That seems awfully expensive, Gracie."

Gracie finally received it for her birthday in November, just after they moved to their new home in the "up-and-coming" neighborhood, as her mother put it. It was Gracie's

only gift for her seventh birthday because of the great expense, but she loved her beading

kit so well that she didn't care if it was her only present for a dozen birthdays. It would be

a hard thing to part with, but it practically guaranteed her a friendship with Odella. Gracie

gathered up the kit, the scotch tape, silver wrapping paper, and a large red bow and took

them to the top of the stairs. It was her favorite place in the new house to do almost

anything because the window at the top of the stairs had a clear view of the rain-swept

Pleasant Avenue which sparkled with the promise of Christmas. A plastic Santa brought his reindeer to a landing on the roof across the street; the baby Jesus was swaddled in a manger just two houses up; and Douglas firs peeked out the front window of almost every home, as if a holiday parade might march around the corner at any moment.

Kneeling in the glow of the twinkling Christmas lights that framed the window, Gracie carefully wrapped her gift, then signed her name to the tag in a flourishing cursive: *From Your Best Friend, Gracie.*

She was just about to go back down the stairs when Nat from next door caught her attention. Nat walked out the front door of the only grey house on the street, which remained conspicuously undecorated for Christmas. She was bundled in her faded green sweater and tattered yellow scarf, and carefully navigated the missing boards on her crooked front porch. As always, she carried a rag doll with her. The same one she dragged to school every day. At least it used to be a doll from what Gracie could tell. She got a

7

good look at it tucked away in Nat's book bag one day at school. The doll was held together with patches of old material, had two mismatched buttons for eyes, a tangle of knotted yarn for hair, and a crooked smile drawn onto its face with black marker. It was even missing an arm. Just the look of that old doll made Gracie shiver for it reminded her of the scary Halloween stories she hated hearing from the boys at her old school.

But what intrigued Gracie on this particular day was not that Nat was carrying the same old doll, but that she was also carrying a bundle of brown paper and knotted twine under one arm. She watched carefully as Nat made it to the bottom stoop of the porch and then walked around to the side yard where she disappeared from view in the overgrown weeds.

Gracie hurried to the bathroom at the end of the hall and looked over the window sill to get a better view of the neighbor's back yard.

Nat wound her way around broken crates, a bathtub, and more than a few rusty old cars, until she finally made her way to a leafless elm tree. Ten feet off the ground, the elm's bony fingers cradled a rickety tree house with a slanted roof and large gaps between the planks that made up its walls. There were a few boards tacked to the trunk of the tree, but far too few to complete a ladder. This fact didn't seem to bother Nat for she slung the doll over one shoulder and scaled the gnarly branches with ease.

Gracie could see Nat as she set the twine and paper down, propped up her doll on an apple crate and pretended to serve tea and cookies from a mismatched yellow and brown tea set. At school, Nat always sat in the back of the classroom never uttering a word. But you'd never guess it by the way she talked now, chatting away with that doll as if they hadn't seen each other in ages. She even seemed to lose her stutter.

Gracie heard the clanking of her mother's utensils and mixing bowls down stairs. Knowing there would be bowls to lick clean of whatever Christmas treat her mother was baking, she raced to the kitchen, losing all interest in the peculiar girl next door.

At school the next day, Gracie scowled at the clock in the front of the classroom for it had been taking its sweet time all day.

"Alright," said Miss Trickle, finally. "You may close your books and put away your things."

A rumble overtook the room as students hastily shoved books in desks and retrieved their Secret Santa gifts from under their seats and inside their backpacks. Gracie couldn't help but notice the gift Odella held on her lap—a gold gift bag embossed with glittering poinsettias, spilling over with green and white tissue paper. It was easily the most beautiful package Gracie had ever seen. When the gifts were all out and the desks closed, everyone sat up straight for they knew Miss Trickle would insist on order before allowing the gift giving to commence.

"Are you sitting up straight, Rufus Minly?" Miss Trickle asked.

All eyes turned to the boy with the messy blond hair and dirty cheeks. Rufus sighed, then reluctantly corrected his slouch.

"Alright then," continued Miss Trickle. "You may take your places around the reading area."

The reading area was carpeted, with a long bookshelf at one end, and surrounded by billowy bean bag chairs. Everyone stampeded toward their favorite spots, elbowing each other to get to the best bean bags as Miss Trickle put away her materials, but they all steered clear of the purple bean bag chair. It was Odella's favorite. The comely girl walked to the reading area fanning out her green Christmas dress with the ruffles on the bottom as she took her place.

All the girls scrambled to sit next to Odella, but Gracie was the quickest, taking a wooden stool with a wobbly leg next to the purple bean bag. When Rufus reached the biggest and smelliest bean bag, he threw his best friend Marcus off with a hard shove and plopped down with a *thwack!* Nat was the last to sit, and the only space available was the floor on the other side of Rufus.

"I ain't sitting next to you," said Rufus to Nat. "Go find somewhere else to sit."

Nat looked around, but there was no place else.

"That's the only seat, Rufus!" challenged Gracie.

"I was just kidding," said Rufus. "Let's see what she's got." Then he swiped Nat's present away from her. It was in a lumpy brown wrapper secured with twine. It had pictures all over it but Gracie couldn't make them out with Rufus swinging it in the air. He held it just out of Nat's reach and croaked, "Jump for it, shrimp."

Gracie looked for Miss Trickle, but the teacher was on the other side of the room, too busy tucking unwieldy hairs back under her bun to notice Rufus. With no other help in sight, Gracie stomped up to the sour-faced boy and planted herself squarely in front of him. "Hand it back," she demanded.

"Or what?"

"Or I'll tell Miss Trickle you put your boogers on the drinking fountain at lunch," she said triumphantly.

Rufus' shoulders drooped. "Fine," he said.

He tossed the package to Nat, but it passed through her arms and fell on the floor. Gracie picked it up, noticing the carefully drawn flowers and trees on the wrapping paper—each flower a different color, each tree with different leaves. "That's very pretty," she said, handing the present to Nat.

The girl clutched the gift tightly to her chest and ran to a faraway chair to sit by herself.

"You're not a nice person," Gracie told Rufus.

"Says you and my mother," hissed Rufus before falling back down onto his stinky bean bag.

13

When Miss Trickle commenced the Secret Santa ceremony, Mary gave a train to Herman, Becky gave a toy dinosaur to Cindy, Billy gave a hockey mask to Valaria, and all the while Gracie rocked back and forth in her rickety stool, anxiously waiting her turn. She imagined the smile spreading across Odella's face, the hug they'd surely share, and how they'd spend all of Christmas break visiting each other's houses.

"Gracie!" said Miss Trickle.

"Yes?" answered Gracie, a little surprised.

"I've been calling on you. It's your turn."

Gracie lifted the carefully wrapped gift and held it out toward Odella. Odella accepted it with a polite smile, then carefully slipped her fingers under the tape and pried the wrapping open—like the way Gracie's grandmother opened gifts so she could save the paper. It was very dignified. When Odella had cleared the paper away, she folded it, placed it beside her, and then opened the wooden box.

"Do you like it?" asked Gracie with a squeak of excitement.

Odella closed the lid, put the beading kit on the floor next to her and said, "It's very thoughtful. Thank you."

And that was it. Nothing else said. Not a smile, or a hug; she didn't even take out any of the beads to see them sparkle in her hand as Gracie had done when she first received the kit.

Gracie faced the class again, very disappointed and more than a little confused. She

14

had ached for that box of treasures, begged her mother and father for months, but Odella Berg acted like it was a box of rocks.

Next it was Odella's turn to give a gift, but even as she stood up with her glittering gift bag, Gracie couldn't stop looking at the box of beads lying on the floor. Discarded. Unappreciated. Lost to a girl who could care less. Odella approached and Gracie forced a polite smile. Maybe Odella's gift would be so amazing that Gracie would forget all about her beading kit, although she couldn't imagine what could possibly be so great. She held out her arms, ready to receive her consolation when Odella passed her by and walked straight to Marla. Marla reached with both hands into the gold bag with the poinsettias and pulled out a white and grey ceramic unicorn, rising up in the air as if it was about to charge.

"Oh, thank you, thank you," gushed Marla. "It's so beautiful. I'm going to put it right by my bed."

It *was* beautiful, and it should have been Gracie's. She could feel her cheeks flush, her hands ball up into fists and it was all she could do not to scream.

15

"You're welcome," said Odella, giving a slight smile before returning to her seat.

"Gracie," said Miss Trickle. "You can take your seat now."

All the other kids laughed. Suddenly Gracie felt stupid, standing there in the middle of the reading area holding back her tears. She walked to the far end of the carpet and squeezed herself between Valaria and Trina so she wouldn't have to sit next to Odella.

"Natalia?" continued Miss Trickle. "Where's Natalia?"

Everyone pointed at the small girl sitting at the back of the room, halfway ducking behind a basketball sized globe—which Rufus was also fond of putting his boogers on.

"Come on, Natalia," Miss Trickle said encouragingly. "It's your turn to give a gift."

Nat hopped off her chair and walked towards the circle of children with her head down. She placed the brown paper package on Gracie's lap, and then walked back to her seat.

Gracie looked after Nat in surprise, then turned to the present—a lumpy mass of brown paper bound with twine. Giggles rattled the room and Gracie looked up to see the whole class gawking at her.

"Hush," Miss Trickle demanded. "That's not polite behavior."

Gracie looked down at the package,

dreading whatever was inside. If the wrapping made the class snicker, the present was sure to make everyone fall over laughing, and then no one would want to be her friend.

She had trouble untying the knotted twine around the package, so Miss Trickle cut the string with scissors. Gracie then pushed aside the homemade wrapping paper and inside found Nat's doll staring at her with its different sized eyes and crooked smile.

All the kids in the class studied the one-armed figure with wide eyes.

"It looks like a voodoo doll," said Marshal.

"It's giving me the spooks," said Cindy.

Odella snatched up the doll and waved it at Nat. "You traded me Gracie's name to give her *this*?"

Everyone laughed, and Nat ran out of the classroom crying.

"That will be enough, Odella," scolded Miss Trickle before running to get Nat. The bell rang as the teacher reached the door and in a matter of moments the room had cleared for Christmas break and no one but Gracie remained.

Gracie heard a strange rolling sound and looked across the classroom floor to see half her beads scurrying away as if they too couldn't wait for Christmas break to begin. She ran to the door to remind Odella not to carry the box sideways. But as she looked out to the school yard she could see Odella laughing with Marshal and Trina as they threw beads at each other and wrapped the colored string around their heads.

Gracie stood there with a lump in her chest until she heard the unmistakable growl of Rufus Minley by the Monkey bars. "Take no prisoners!" he shouted.

She turned to see Rufus and Markus fighting over Nat's ragdoll, its stuffing falling to the ground in clumps as they tugged it every which way. Gracie rushed to rescue it, but by the time she reached the tetherball court, the doll had been reduced to a pile of cloth. She spied Nat hiding in a nearby bush, tears in her eyes as she stared at what used to be her doll, and in that moment Gracie realized that Nat had loved her doll just as much as Gracie had loved her beading kit.

Gracie walked up to the neighbor's grey house the next day. It looked haunted with its dark windows, crooked roof, and smoke puffing out of three different places on the chimney where bricks were missing. She clutched a brown paper package to her chest that she had decorated herself with drawings of butterflies and a waterfall. She walked through the muddy yard, then carefully made her way across the porch.

Before Gracie could even knock, a dark figure appeared on the other side of the dusty screen door. "What do you want?" said an old woman's voice.

Gracie was so frightened that the words stuck in her throat.

"Well?" insisted the woman.

"I—I'm looking for Nat," she finally had the courage to say.

"Oh, you're the new neighbor. You must mean Natalia."

"Yes, ma'am."

"Well, she ain't never in here," said the woman. "She's probably out back."

Then the dark figure stepped back and the door slammed.

Gracie made her way to the back yard, remembering the path she had seen Nat take. By the time she got to the elm tree, the bottom of her dress was covered in mud and her sleeve had snagged on a rusty car bumper. She could see Nat through the walls of the tree house, sitting on a stool in front of the mismatched tea set and staring at the empty apple crate that used to be her doll's chair.

Gracie put her package under one arm and climbed the tree as she had seen Nat do, although it took her a bit longer. She popped her head through the opening in the floor and pulled herself up and in, then sat on the floor next to Nat who had hardly moved a muscle.

"Hi," said Gracie.

"H—H—Hi," said Nat.

"You ran away. I didn't get to say thank you."

"It's ok—k—kay, I know you didn't like my present."

"I did like it," said Gracie. "I'm sorry the boys got to it."

Nat stared at the ground and Gracie scooted across the floor so she could face her easily. "Why did you trade Odella's name for mine?" she asked.

Nat looked down at Gracie as if it was a silly question. "C—c—cause you're my best friend."

At that moment, Gracie felt ashamed for trying so hard to win Odella's friendship when Nat's friendship was right there in front of her. Ashamed for not appreciating Nat's

20

gift enough to keep it out of the hands of two dirt-faced boys. At the same time, she was also happy that Nat considered her a friend.

She put the package on Nat's lap and said, "This is for you."

"For what?" asked Nat.

"Because I should have traded Odella's name for yours."

Nat smiled, then began to gingerly undo the wrapping on her present.

"No, like this," said Gracie. Then she stood up and ripped open one side of the wrapping. Nat smiled and did the same, and soon the two girls were giggling as they shredded the wrapping and flakes of paper fell down around them like confetti.

Nat finally caught her breath and lifted the lid on the cigar box in her lap. Her eyes widened to take in all the colors of string and different sizes of beads.

"I picked up all the pieces that Odella dropped and added a few ribbons of my own. The box isn't as nice as the one I gave Odella but—"

"I think it's perfect!" Nat gasped. "We can make necklaces and bracelets and headbands and … and …." Nat paused, her eyes turning sad. "But won't Odella w-want them back?"

"I don't think so," said Gracie. "Besides, these are for my best friend, Nat."

Nat smiled so broadly that Gracie could hardly count the teeth. She hugged Gracie and said, "by the way, my name's Natalia. A Nat is a b-bug. I don't like bugs."

All of Christmas break, until the sun went down, Gracie and Natalia played and chatted away the hours in the tree house. They even decorated it with tinsel and ornaments for Christmas and New Year's. And in the spring they drew bunnies on the walls and hid

eggs in the corners; in the fall they hoisted pumpkins up the tree and carved them into

scary faces; and year after year   they played, and laughed, and

cried together, like   best friends should.

ABOUT THE AUTHOR

P. A. Navarro resides in Portland, Oregon where he lives with his wife and cats. The Gift Giver was written sometime in the way-back past, but it was dusted off and polished up to serve as his first published story. His middle-grade novel, The Incredible Misadventures of Zadora Zane will be released soon. For further information, please go to www.panavarro.com.

www.ingramcontent.com/pod-product-compliance
Lightning Source LLC
Chambersburg PA
CBHW041008170626
46815CB00002B/213